D1590764

Annemarie Nikolaus

Falling for a Movie Star

Quick, quick, slow – Lietzensee Dance Club

Novel

1

With her freaky bicycle bell Tanja Walters startled two magpies, which were bickering over a glittering shred of tinfoil paper on the bike path. The paper got left behind as the two of them fled into the chestnut tree in front of the fairground at Berlin-Zehlendorf's Hüttenweg.

Tanja got off and locked her bike to a streetlamp. Then she bent down for the tinfoil and threw it in the next trashcan. Served them right!

Each merry-go-round had a different music playing; the operators apparently tried to drown out one another. Did they think who was loudest attracted the most people?

The seductive scent of grilled food was wafting towards her. Fairground visitors crowded into an alleyway lined with barbecue stalls with corn, grill ribs, steaks and American beer. She just came from lunch, but she still would have bought at least one rib, if the lines in front of the food stalls hadn't been that long.

For her as a square dancer, the German-American Folk Festival was a must. And she loved it. The real America she could afford only, when she was done with her architecture studies.

At the Ferris wheel she met the first one from the Lietzensee Dance Club: Norbert Kaminski was just getting out of a gondola with his twelve-year-old son Oliver.

"Tanja, Tanja!" Oliver hopped towards her. "Will you ride the ghost train with me?"

"Why me?" She grinned at Norbert. "Is your father afraid?"

Oliver pulled the corners of his mouth down. "No. That's why it's no fun with Dad. He's just pretending."

"Then you'll have to come back when your mother's around. I'm not scared either."

"I can't do that." Suddenly Oliver looked like he was about to burst into tears.

Norbert raised his eyebrows warningly. Apparently she'd put her foot in her mouth. And she thought Norbert's divorce had been consensual.

She put her arm around Oliver's shoulders. "Then we'll make Chris do it. Come on, let's go find him."

They had arranged to meet the others from their square dance group on "Main Street". Here the owners of the stalls had agreed on country music. Very sensible! It was a little quieter, too. Tanja sang along with what she knew as they looked for the dancers.

Chris Rinehart, the group's American caller, stood next to Tanja's partner Micky Hassloff at a shooting gallery. Chris was dressed in plain clothes, while Micky looked like a cowboy from his Stetson to the high-heeled boots. A very authentic-looking cowboy: muscular and tanned, as if he were actually herding cattle all year round. Even the sand blond hair looked like being bleached by too much sun. In reality, he sat day and night at the University of Technology in front of some stupid computers.

Chris was instructing him in the use of an air gun and the shooting gallery's owner followed their actions with obvious displeasure. But then he got distracted by an older man wearing a sombrero and a fringed trapper shirt and turned away from them.

She approached and then pointed to the owner. "I guess he's afraid Micky's gonna clear out his stall."

Micky turned around. The blue of his eyes became more intense as he looked at her. Dark as a lake she could sink into. What a silly thought! She'd drown; she couldn't even swim.

She leaned with an elbow on the counter next to him hoping she looked cool.

"Tanja, what can I shoot you?"

"For me? Well... Not a stuffed animal, anyway. I already have a hundred of them. At least." She looked from the running belt with the numbers rolling past to the prizes on display and back to the running belt. "Can you even know beforehand what you're gonna score?"

Chris laughed. "Well, somehow he'll hit something."

"Something..." It was all bells and whistles that was lined up. "Can't they let you win something useful?" Maybe she had better tell Micky right away that she wasn't interested in any of this stuff. But he must have already paid for his shots. And he shouldn't think she didn't want anything from him.

"This here is the German-American Folk Festival!" Micky swung the air gun. "This is not a matter of utility, but of peace of nations. Or something like that."

"Peace of nations? Micky, you fell out of time: The GDR no longer exists." As always, when he could not come up with an answer, he got red ears. It was so easy to rag him.

"You mean our way of life." Chris pointed with a similarly pompous gesture as Micky to the alley with the barbecues.

"Your way of life? Pah!" She grinned cheekily. "You just copied our quadrille."

"But you have to admit, our square dance is much funnier than your quadrille. That's why it's long gone out of fashion." Chris put one hand on Micky's back. "The longer you hesitate, the more insecure you'll become."

Micky's gaze went from the running belt back to Tanja. "That

7

can't be! More insecure is impossible." Especially when she was so close to him that her perfume was fogging him. As if just the sight of her wasn't enough to take his breath away. Her dark blond hair had just grown back to half length and it stroked her face with every gust of wind. There, on her cheek, he'd like to have his own fingers. But there was probably nothing he could do about it. They had been dancing together for over three years now, but Tanja didn't even come to him when she couldn't get along with her computer.

With an eye pinched, he put the rifle against his shoulder, decided on a target and shot. Missed. What did he let Chris sweet-talk him into it! He reloaded and shot a second time without aiming for long. This time he scored. He straightened and wiped his clammy fingers on his pants. "Coincidence." At least now he didn't look like a complete idiot.

But he still had two shots left to embarrass himself. He leveled the gun again; both times he hit a number on the running belt. Grinning with relief, he put the gun on the counter and looked at the owner expectantly. "Now I'm curious." Judging by the owner's sinister face, he had just shot a few decent wins.

Tanja grabbed his arm and pulled him around. "Hit three out of four times. Micky, you're a natural."

Thereupon he didn't know anything to say. Self-conscious, he turned his gaze back to the owner of the stall.

But Chris added another one. "I told you so in the first place. You accomplish what you're setting out to do."

His neck became hot; he must be blushing now. He kept a stubborn gaze on the owner, who was arranging winnings back and forth. "He doesn't seem to know what to give me." And louder. "Young man, may I choose something, or how does that work now?"

"Just a moment," came the grumpy answer. All of a sudden the man no longer had an American accent, but a tonality that sounded very Hessian.

"Despite the hat and the clothes: That's not an American." Tanja smirked openly. "Americans are much more generous.

Chris laughed and patted her on the back. "I'm honored, ma'am."

The owner of the shooting gallery finally settled on handing over the prizes. Of course one of them was an oversized stuffed animal – a pink version of Bugs Bunny.

Micky tried to saddle Oliver with it, but he refused outraged. "Pink is for girls!"

Chris finally took the rabbit from him: Madeline could make her grandmother happy with it. The second prize was soap bubbles; Oliver accepted them graciously. The third prize, on the other hand, had a certain merit: a steam iron. But how could he give such a thing to Tanja?

She unpacked it and looked at it from all sides. "For my mother!"

"Do you think she'll iron my shirts to thank me?"

"My mother never irons!" Arrogantly she raised her chin.

He stared at her. Did she really think he was serious about his question?

Laughter lines crinkled around her eyes as she swiveled the iron. "Maybe she'll start now." She pulled his leg! And he had once again fallen for it. How did she always do that?

"Let the man check if it works," Chris warned.

"I didn't know you could be so finicky." Madeline Lagrange's voice suddenly sounded behind them.

Chris turned around, pulled her close and kissed her persistently.

"You obviously want me to want us to finish the tour!

Before I even started?" Madeline laughed, half out of breath from the long kiss.

"What?" Chris made an innocent face as if he didn't understand what she meant. "We have something to do first."

Tanja handed the iron to the shooting gallery's owner for testing. But without distilled water there was little to try; at least it turned on and became hot. Which meant she couldn't wrap it up right away. She shoved it into Micky's hand and he had to carry it until it cooled down.

Tanja linked arms with Norbert and took Oliver by the hand. They followed Chris to a stage where three men were sitting in front of an electric campfire playing Western songs on their guitars. At least one of them sang rather off-key.

"Boo!" Insouciant as usual, Tanja made no secret of her disgust. "Some things here are really an imposition."

Oliver inclined his head. "They are yowling. I think your dance music is better."

Norbert laughed and tousled Oliver's hair. "You and Tanja obviously have the same taste, cowboy."

Chris climbed the steps near the stage and disappeared behind a curtain. Shortly afterwards he came out with a radiant face, next to him a young man with a cigar in the corner of his mouth. The man said something;, then Chris tapped around on his cell and shook the man's hand.

He jumped down to them with one leap. "Werner will be thrilled. We'll get 500 euros."

Madeline frowned. "Who – for what?"

"We for a performance here."

"Great." Micky patted Chris on the back. "It will strengthen our position in the club."

Tanja smirked. "Not even the Latin formation brings that much. As little as he takes us seriously; Gorge can't afford to waste us."

"Grandpa's just old-fashioned; but he only means well with the club."

"Old-fashioned?" Micky made a face. That Madeline was still defending her grandfather... "I only say 'quadrille'." George Lagrange wasn't even interested in the old dances his wife was researching.

Madeline was still a little incredulous looking from one to the other. "You mean, our square dance group will dance here? But we're not Americans at all." In the few months that she danced with them, she had not yet seen how strange some performances came about.

"Since the Army left, it has become more difficult to have these fairs genuinely American. Or it is expensive." Chris pointed to the singers who just bowed at the edge of the stage. "Not authentic either."

On stage the next number began: a group of dancers dressed as saloon girls. They were really good and were applauded also by the female spectators when they turned around at the end and lifted their skirts.

"This cancan isn't quite in style either, is it?" Unexpectedly Madeline grabbed Chris by the arm and pulled him around with a violent movement. "Did you make an appointment?" She suddenly seemed to panic about being up there herself. Of course; it would be her first public appearance with them. "Without knowing if everyone has time to dance? What about Hinnerk? He's in Hong Kong again..."

Chris put his hand on her mouth to calm her down. "Easy!" He kissed her fleetingly on the cheek. "Don't get worked up. The manager has suggested three different dates. We don't have to take them all."

"But then there will be less money," Tanja said. She should be elected to the board; then the club would have no more worries.

Micky quickly turned to the side so she wouldn't see his grin. Maybe she would feel offended.

"Of course. What did you think? Every gig is paid extra." Chris was still hugging Madeline and stroking her back. The two were a sight to be envied.

"Then we should dance three times." Micky winked at Tanja. "And put Madeline's grandfather out of action for all time."

"Out of action?" She pushed him into the side. "You've really adapted well to the Wild West."

"I am capable of learning; don't you know that?" He grinned mischievously.

She looked at him skeptically. But this time he didn't fall for it. He raised his chin confidently and thereupon she had no line at the ready.

2

Five days later Micky was again standing with Tanja and fourteen other square dancers in front of the stage at the German-American Folk Festival.

This time Chris, like all other men, wore high-heeled cowboy boots, Stetson and Bolo Tie with jeans and checkered shirts. The ladies dressed in knee-length skirts in bright colors and lavish petticoats; not contemporary for the Wild West, but meanwhile the customary costume for square dancing. Tanja had Carola Maaßen put her hair up; a few curly strands framed her face. She looked even more enchanting than usual.

Lydia Aydemir's musically challenged husband had faithfully come to applause, as had Norbert's entire crowd of children, including their mother. Bettina Hinz's husband carried their daughter in the baby sling on his chest; she slept completely unimpressed by the noise of the fair. Andrea Falshagen's husband had at least been able to persuade the adolescent daughter to come along; the other two children meanwhile went their own ways, which did not lead them to the Lietzensee Dance Club.

One of the Berlin clubs specializing in square dancing danced before them. A fiddler duo who worked for the stage accompanied them. They weren't authentic either: The two men played the violin, not the fiddle.

"On average, they are much older than our group," remarked Norbert, who, at thirty-five, was himself no longer one of the youngest. "They lack suppleness."

"Quite contrary to you." With a flash of her eyes the old-fashioned kind - flirting brand Western style - Carola, his partner, linked arms with him.

Norbert's ex-wife audibly gasped in outrage, but then she was taken over by her two little daughters. She hadn't wanted him anymore, but she was still jealous. Who could understand the women! Micky shook his head over her.

But it was not only suppleness that the other group lacked. Nothing grave, and yet... They were lacking in harmony, in accuracy. As if they were at odds or constantly competing with each other. The applause was sparse; very clearly only polite, not enthusiastic. Even the untrained eyes of the audience probably hadn't missed the slip-ups.

Madeline turned to Chris. "We have the better caller."

He kissed her nonchalantly and stroked her back to dampen her stage fright. This late July afternoon was still oppressively hot; but it was hardly due to the heat that Madeline's dress was already sticking to her back, soaked in sweat.

Norbert pushed Chris into the side. The stage manager was – cigar in the corner of his mouth – on his way to them.

Micky reached for Tanja, but instead of climbing up to the stage with him, she linked arms with Madeline.

"Do you have stage fright?" she asked. All right; under these circumstances he didn't have to interpret that as rejection.

Madeline swallowed heavily and didn't bring out a sound; she pressed a hand to her chest.

"I don't know you like that at all," Tanja said. But it was the first time that Madeline appeared with them in public. "Don't fret. It will work out!"

Chris stopped right behind the curtain and had the manager attach a wireless microphone. As Madeline walked past him to her position in the square, he breathed a kiss on her cheek. "You look like a corpse, darling."

"Well, thank you. Great compliment!"

"You'll feel better in a moment." He held her and kissed her on the mouth, his eyes glittering with mischief.

Chris' bubbly mood seemed contagious. Exuberantly Tanja reached for Micky's hand and spun into his arm before they lined up properly. The flaming gaze she threw at him in the process took his breath away momentarily: Didn't it resemble the one Madeline had just had for Chris? But certainly he had only imagined it.

The curtain went up and the manager introduced them. Chris raised his hand; the violinists started the first piece of music and Chris sang his calls: "Bow to the partner. Join and circle to the left for a while... Walk around the corner..."

As Tanja swung her skirts during the "walk", the scent that surrounded her became more intense. Her mother had used fabric softener once again. Micky tried desperately to suppress the sneezing stimulus. "Circulate... And swing your girl..." He took her into a dancing posture and for a moment she leaned into his arm before following his gentle pressure into the movement. When she danced with him, they became one and Tanja knew what he wanted from her a second before his next signal. But as soon as the music faded, she was distant and sarcastic.

Then their performance was over. From the spectators came downright frenetic applause. The audience hadn't clapped that much for the other square dancers. Tanja exhaled a long gasp as if she had held her breath. Although she had performed so many times before, every time the fear that she might blunder it, seemed to seize her again. Without comment, she accepted him taking her by the hand and stroking the back of her hand with his thumb.

He pulled her to the edge of the stage. "Bow!"

Then the curtain slid between them and the audience. The manager pointed to a box of mineral water cans and Micky took out two for himself and Tanja.

Madeline wiped the sweat off her forehead with her arm. "Is it always so nerve-racking?"

Carola laughed. "And it's not even a competition."

"Who would know!" Norbert had found a beer and was sporting now a foam beard in his face. He did without the steps and jumped from the stage directly in front of his son, who had waited there for the end of the performance.

Oliver jumped up and down. "Are we going to the roller coaster now, Dad? Jasmin and Maike have made it twice already."

"Of course! We'll catch up immediately." Norbert pushed his Stetson into his nape and with a wide grin he took his leave. With his hand on Oliver's back, he shoved him through the crowd.

Micky was still holding Tanja's hand as they descended the stairs. Suddenly it made her nervous. "I won't get lost." She pulled her hand away.

He looked at her in bewilderment; then he shrugged.

Chris came down the steps next to the stage, engrossed in lively conversation with a massive man with light hair. His suit was too expensive for a fairground man. He seemed familiar to her, but she just had no idea where to put him. A politician?

Chris reached out to Madeline and pulled her to himself. "Madeline, please meet Ralph Kincaid."

Kincaid, the film producer! No Senate jerk. Exactly; she had seen the man on some TV show.

"Ralph, meet Madeline Lagrange." Chris pronounced her last name in French, not in Berlin dialect. So it sounded much more elegant; Tanja smothered her grin. "She's the granddaughter of one of the heads." What heads? Of what?

"I would never brag about Grandpa," Madeline said to Chris in German. They were speaking of the Lietzensee Dance Club?

Kincaid didn't seem to have understood her. "Nice to meet you, Miss."

Then he turned to Chris again. He obviously only spoke English. "Your troupe convinced me, Chris."

Tanja approached. "Convinced of what?" She didn't bother to hide her misgivings.

Kincaid turned to her. "Your troupe is the best of all I've seen these days."

"You're interested in something like that, Mister Kincaid?"

"Ralph, please." He turned to Madeline again: "Miss... Madeline, do you think your grandfather could take time for me today or tomorrow?" Well, that one was in a hurry!

"Why do you want to see Grandpa, Ralph?"

"Because I want ho have you. I expect three days of shooting."

Tanja gasped. "Days of shooting? You want to hire us for a movie?" Incredible. "Los Alamos!" That was it! That's why Kincaid looked so familiar to her. "Manolo Rioja is shooting 'Los Alamos' in Babelsberg. And you're the producer, aren't you?" That couldn't be real; she was dreaming.

Madeline burst out laughing. "Why do you have such good knowledge, Tanja?"

"Well, came in all detail at *rbb*." Her hands became

clammy with excitement. "Manolo Rioja is the leading actor. It will be a really beautiful classic Western..."

Chris interrupted her with a gesture of his hand. "Tell us later in the pub."

"Your enthusiasm is a big compliment to us." Kincaid pulled his cell from his jacket pocket, stared at it and typed a quick answer. Then he turned to Tanja again. "I'll tell you everything you want to know about the movie."

"A Western?" Madeline looked incredulously from her to Kincaid. "You're shooting a Western in Germany?"

"It pays off. Your country has great film funding." He grinned. "And you get almost everything here. Background actors for the square dance shots, for example." He put his cell back. "Only for the scenes outside of Los Alamos our scouts didn't find a suitable location. We'll shoot them in France."

Out of excitement Tanja got a dry mouth; she shouldn't have left the mineral water can behind the stage. "Background actors. You probably need a lot of them in a Western like that."

Kincaid scrutinized her from top to bottom. Did he wonder if he could use her?

She hastily added: "During the semester breaks, I'm earning for my studies as a background actress." In fact, she had only done it twice and only for television; cinema, that was certainly another number. But she didn't have to tell him that.

"How many of our people do you want to hire?" As always, Madeline was more interested in practical considerations; she didn't seem to be particularly fond of actors.

"I want to have three squares. Two couples of actors and background actors will come from the set. Will you be able to manage that, Chris?"

"Can these actors dance anything?" Chris asked.

Kincaid shrugged. "It will be enough. It's realistic that not everyone is equally good. And we won't fully focus on them."

"That's daring, Chris! If even one of our substitute dancers misses, the whole affair will crash." Madeline obviously wanted to talk him out of it. Oh no! Tanja threw her a grim look. She wouldn't miss that on any account.

But before she could think of anything to say, Chris came to her aid. "Don't worry, darling. What do we have a whole club for?" Soothingly he stroked Madeline's back.

"I don't think we can get other people from the club. Grandpa will be afraid that we'll alienate them from him."

Micky shrugged. "On the quiet..."

"Exactly!" Tanja looked at him gratefully. Micky was the best! "And I bring my brother. Axel is used to being ordered around by me." Switching to English, she turned to Kincaid again. "When do you want to start?"

"In four weeks we'll start shooting," he replied.

"Maybe our circle will get a little bigger afterwards and we can eventually open a third square." Now Madeline actually seemed to find something good in the whole thing.

"Which means, again nobody can afford to miss." Carola smirked. "You've done a nice job, Chris."

"I know of at least one substitute dancer who would like to have a permanent place in the square."

Everyone laughed, looking at Madeline: Since several months she often had to stand at the sidelines during practice, because Bettina, Hinnerk's real partner, was dancing again since the end of her maternity leave. To make up for it, Tanja and Carola alternately left their partners to her, but of course that wasn't the solution.

Grinning, Chris put his arm around Madeline, "I'll give you some extra coaching until the shooting."

3

Two weeks before shooting began, Kincaid informed Chris that they had now engaged the background actors for square dancing. Thereupon Chris moved the Tuesday practice to Babelsberg to integrate the two unknown couples into the group.

Micky picked Tanja up at the Institute of Architecture at Ernst-Reuter-Platz. She had done something with her hair and her face was framed by little curls. The skirt, which ended just above the knees, was lavish enough to replace the square dance costume if they didn't find an opportunity to change that afternoon.

His knees went mellow as she greeted him with unexpected vehemence. He lowered his face into her hair and wanted to put his arms around her waist, but she grabbed his hand. "Come!" She pulled him across the foyer to a showcase. "I designed that," she said proudly. "Do you like it?"

If only he knew what that was supposed to be! A high tower, which had a certain resemblance to a mushroom, only that the glass "head" consisted of four parts, which were connected together only at the trunk. Very strange. "Very ingenious." He smiled timidly. "Certainly up there you feel like you're sitting outdoors."

"Precisely. That's the way it's meant to be." Tanja beamed even more than before, obviously delighted with his answer.

"And what is it?"

She frowned. "How - what? A skyscraper, of course."

Of course. "Will this get built?"

"Silly! This is a seminar project. Sometimes they don't even build projects that won a competition." Abruptly she turned away; had he said something wrong again? But she only pointed to the clock hanging under the ceiling. "Off to... battle."

They met Axel and the other dancers at the entrance to the studios in Babelsberg. In addition to the address of the studio Chris had received a small map from Kincaid. Not evident from it was that it took ages to walk from one end of the site to the other. Which was why everybody drove while they had parked their cars at the entrance. Actually, they could have imagined it.

"But this is great here!" Tanja had a reverential expression on her face as she looked around attentively. "These production sets — somebody has to design them. I wonder if I could suggest to my professor to build a movie town for once."

Axel grinned. "You could persuade an elephant to fly... That shouldn't be a problem either."

"It is. There is a postgraduate course in 'Stage Design — Scenic Space'. That's where he could push the idea. But that's only for theater and exhibitions, not for movie sets." Tanja with self-doubt — that was something completely new. Was that why she had asked his opinion about her design? And he had shown so little enthusiasm; she was certainly disappointed by him.

After ten minutes they reached an alley with two-story wooden facades: the Western Town. "If we had such a project in the design seminar, maybe it would even be built. And that would be something solid for once."

Micky linked arms with her. "But not exactly long-lasting." Ugh; that sounded wrong. Hopefully she didn't think now he wanted to talk her out of it. "Just like we do with our cyber worlds. Only virtually for eternity." That probably wasn't any better either; he'd rather not say anything anymore.

The street in front of them seemed to consist of compacted sandy soil, but certainly there was a real tarmac road underneath. The top layer of sand was stirred up by gusts of wind. Someplace there were blowers installed, which probably even created a storm when needed.

Two women with sweeping feather hats were cycling past them. A van parked in front of the saloon and two men dragged crates of drinks into the building. At its back there was a pen with four beautiful, relatively small horses.

Kincaid's office was at the "exit" of the Western Town. A flippant dispatcher behind a computer pointed Chris curtly to the studio building opposite, which had been rented for "Los Alamos".

"Kind people here." Tanja spoke so loudly that the dispatcher had to hear her. The girl turned red. When Tanja talked about her TV shots, it always sounded as if the people there were like one big family. Apparently not everyone on this set belonged to it. But the dispatcher now knew that they expected respect.

Micky was still smirking when he opened the heavy studio door for Tanja. Glistening spotlights blinded him after a few steps. They stood in front of a sort of living room with a large open fireplace in which a fire was burning. Still, it was cooler than outside; the air conditioning even compensated for the heat from the spotlights. None of the cameras were running; they were probably only rehearsing.

The man in the elegant black suit was Manolo Rioja, the leading actor. He stood by the fireplace with a half-filled whiskey glass in his hand and stared angrily at a man in worn, dirty cowboy clothes. An impressive contrast that immediately clarified the relationship between the two men. Rioja spoke Spanish, the other one English. Interesting. Apparently, everyone had a script in their own language – what an effort.

Chris had found Kincaid and now guided them past the scene through a narrow corridor into another studio room. In the middle of it stood a large wooden platform; otherwise the room was empty except for a table with a small music system.

Kincaid introduced a gray haired man as Assistant Director to them. Jack Harten would take care of everything they needed. Then Kincaid disappeared.

An older woman and a young man leaned against the wall and talked quietly. Harten wanted to start the rehearsals without the missing second couple and waved them over: "Emily" – Beate Schäfer – and "Terence" – Franz Daubert – would come from one of the ranches to Los Alamos for the festival.

Chris set up two squares to show the two background actors the calls with which the dance would begin. He let Axel dance with them right away, because Tanja had already shown him the intended figures at home. As an exception, there was actually a fixed sequence. "Bow to your partners... and promenade... circle to the right..." Chris didn't sing the calls as usual; it was bemusing.

After that Chris asked the two background actors to replace Lydia and Norbert. The beginning was simple enough; after the second repetition he was satisfied and went on to the next calls. Again he had the figures demonstrated first, then the background actors replaced Tanja and Hinnerk.

Disappointed, Tanja leaned against the wall next to Chris. How boring this started here. Just a good deed for the budget of the club. She had been naïve to think that she would get to know Manolo Rioja.

"You are an excellent teacher, Tanja. – Double pass thru." Chris pointed to Axel while the dancers passed each other in a circle. "Can't you convince him to get in with us? – First couple go left. Next couple go left."

"He rather stops attending the dance circle as well. His band is more important to him right now."

"... and promenade..." Arm in arm the couples were walking the circle. This Beate was downright leaning into Micky's shoulder... If she wasn't so much older than him, she would suspect the woman of hitting at him. Or did she actually?

Then Chris sent her and Hinnerk back to their squares and had Madeline and Simon Hülter drop out.

When they started the fourth part of the calls, Rioja came in, followed by a teenage girl. Out of excitement, Tanja took a wrong breath and began to cough.

Rioja looked even more gorgeous than in the movies; she would have expected it the other way. The silver threads in his black hair and the gray temples were dyed for the part to make him look like in his late fifties. Yet he was the best-looking man she had ever met. And now she had him in front of her for real.

"Impressive." She stared at Rioja and promptly missed the next step. Micky had to get her moving with an energetic push. Bewildered, he kept his hand on her hip longer than necessary and then was half a beat late himself.

Rioja watched the dance. Did he look at her more often than at the others? Again and again she looked at him, but she couldn't figure it out.

Shortly thereafter she was once more out of sync with the movements of the others and arrived too late in the middle of the square.

"Where are your eyes?" Micky whispered in her ear as she stood next to him again. "Concentrate, please."

She nodded and turned her gaze off Rioja. Hopefully he hadn't noticed her blunder. How embarrassing that would be!

In the next dance break Rioja approached Chris. "I'm supposed to dance with you. Instruct me, please." So he and the girl were the missing couple for the third square.

This was the chance of her life! If she were fast enough now to create *faits accomplis*... She gave Micky a push. "Off with you! You are our best dancer to be borrowed! Take care of the little one."

Micky rolled his eyes. "This loaning becomes a habit for you. What is that supposed to tell me?"

She grinned at him. "That I am generous? Jealousy is a foreign word to me?"

He burst out laughing. "As if that girl could even come close to you." All of a sudden he blushed and turned quickly to Chris. "Tell us!"

Chris let him stay in his position and sent the girl to him. Tanja moved to Axel in the square where Rioja was supposed to dance. It could hardly have gone any better. Only with some effort did she suppress the grin that wanted to spread across her face.

Shortly afterwards Rioja stood next to her in the circle and grabbed her hand at "circle left". His fingers were rough, as if he worked regularly with his hands. How did someone like him get calluses?

She scrutinized him more closely. His black hair was styled with a center parting, which gave him a very old-fashioned look. The dark five o'clock shadow was certainly real; but had he been wearing a mustache lately, or was it affixed? It had been a while since she had seen an interview with him.

He was little known in Germany; there were hardly any Western movies left in the cinema.

Beate, Franz and the young girl named Ana, who came from Madrid, asked to be shown some steps once more after the end of the scheduled rehearsal. But Rioja left before Tanja could even say a word to him. Why was he in such a hurry? He was the star after all; he could certainly schedule the rehearsals as he saw fit.

Micky grabbed her by her shoulder and tore her out of her thoughts. "Let's go."

Chris waved his car key invitingly, the other hand around Madeline's waist. "For today we are finished here. See you at the club on Friday."

"Go ahead; I want to have some look at this here." And she didn't want Micky to be with her. "Carola, what about you?"

Of course Carola didn't let her down; she was her best friend after all. But the tour was boring. One studio building next to the other; they didn't interest Tanja. More scenery that reminded her of the Arena of Verona, where the stage sets stood outside too, when they were not needed. No trace of Rioja. Eventually she gave up and they walked towards the exit.

Carola stopped abruptly. "Look at that. A queue like in front of the employment office."

"And it's one; in a way." "Casting Office" read above the front door.

They continued strolling. Carola pointed to the huge poster hanging at the next studio building. "Impressive!" It had rather the character of a painting than a movie billboard and showed a battle from a time when there still was cavalry. One of those crowd scenes.

Crowd scenes! That was brilliant! Tanja stopped.

"Come; I have an idea!" She grabbed Carola's arm and tried to pull her back to the casting office.

Carola braced herself against the pressure of Tanja's hand. "What are you up to?"

"I want to find out something ."

Carola pushed her hand aside. "If you act so mysteriously, I won't go with you."

"Maybe they need more background actors for 'Los Alamos'." Surely she would then find a better opportunity to get to know Rioja than during square dancing.

"We have enough dancers."

"Not as dancers. People. Bar girls. What do I know."

Carola stared at her another moment, then it dawned on her. Finally! "You want to apply?"

"We do!" She pulled at Carola's arm again. "With an extra performance you could improve your budget quite nicely. It's illogical, anyway, not to have square dancers walking through the scenes on other occasions as well. They're dancing at a celebration or something, so that must be the people who live in Los Alamos."

"You might be right. But we shouldn't go through this casting office, we should talk to Kincaid or Harten."

"You're a real friend, Carola." Delighted, she threw her arms around her neck. "You're right; there's a better chance they'll take us. After all, at the employment office, they never have a clue about anything."

"There is only one problem: 'We', that doesn't work. I can't put my apprenticeship at risk."

"But you could do with the money!" She looked at her pleadingly. "And you don't enjoy the apprenticeship anyway."

"But the work itself." She reached for Tanja's hair and pulled a strand out of her hairstyle. "Would you look so smart on your head without me? – But the wage." Carola sighed.

"And the customers." She pressed her lips together. But she came along anyway.

Back in the studio they found Kincaid. Once again entertained by Tanja's enthusiasm, he agreed. He also understood that Carola had reservations because of her apprenticeship, but would actually like to become involved. He found a solution for that too: After all, Carola regularly had a day off during the week.

Tanja bragged brazenly about her poor television experience and got an individual performance: In the role of a young farmer's daughter Tanja was supposed to do some shopping in Los Alamos. Later, during the attack on the festival, she would fall victim to an Indian arrow. Unfortunately, she was not to die in Rioja's arms, but she would think of something.

Carola got a scene at the bar where a girl was missing due to an accident.

4

Hot and cramped: Three hours before the shooting started, Tanja entered the dressing room for the extra girls, Carola intimidated behind her. The air was stuffy; there was no window and the air conditioning seemed overtaxed on this extremely hot day.

Two women helped others to tie up corsets and to put on clothes. Three more sat in front of large mirrors. One of them just removed her make-up; the other two were made up, while at the same time two hairdressers put their hair up and curled it.

None of them looked as if it was their job to organize anything here.

"Make room, please!" A young woman rolled a rack full of clothes through the door.

Tanja took a step to the side and bumped against a chair. "Say..." She grabbed the woman's arm. "We're new; who's in charge here?"

The woman let go of her clothes rack. "Who are you?"

"I am Tanja Walters and..."

The woman interrupted her with a snort. "Who you are! Not what your names are."

"Oh well, yes." How could she have been so thoughtless; her face began to blaze with embarrassment. "I am the farmer's daughter Susan Miller and Carola... is the bar girl Daisy."

The woman turned to Carola and scrutinized her from top to bottom. "Size 40?" Carola made a face as if she had been slapped. She was certainly annoyed that she had not kept up her diet again. "The clothes for the girls are hanging over there. There should be one that fits you."

Carola went to the hangers on the wall and began to check the clothes.

"And you, Tanja, you are Susan? I'll get your costume from the pool. Take off your clothes in the meantime." Before she left, she turned to one of the hairdressers and explained to her what she should do with Tanja and Carola.

While Carola was being made up, she seemed more interested in the woman who was doing Tanja's hair than in her own make-up: She watched attentively every move with which the hairdresser gave Tanja's half-length hair the impression of more opulence and length. Again Carola surely didn't dare to open her mouth, although Tanja nodded to her encouragingly.

So she began to ask the hairdresser herself: They found out that she was permanently employed in Babelsberg and responsible for the background actors. The stars often brought their own staff with them, because their appearance and outfitting were of course given much more attention.

An hour later their hair was done, they were made up and in their costumes. Above three petticoats Carola wore a sea blue dress with a deep neckline and many frills. Carola had cursed unrestrainedly at the first glance at the dress, but surprisingly it didn't make her look fat, it made her look more feminine. Tanja, in contrast, looked poor in her simple gray linen dress; but the hat she had to wear was pretty.

In Tanja's scene "Susan" had to drop off the shopping list at the store and then bring in her cowboy to upload. She would find him in the saloon, which she had expected. But not that he was about to go to a room with a dancer. The following argument with the cowboy then turned into a general brawl.

Carola sat on the bench in front of the sheriff's office, while the outside shot for the sequence with Tanja was rehearsed. In front of the store "Susan's" cart was standing with the horse. It was obviously only a temporary help too, because it reacted increasingly agitated to the shooting operation.

Tanja's task for the beginning of the scene was quite simple: She had – invisible to the camera – to open the shop door from the inside. Then she would stop for a moment on the sidewalk, look around for the cowboy, go down the stairs with gathered skirts, whilst watching out for him and then walk across the street to the saloon.

Tanja went into the store. In the real Los Alamos it was certainly no hotter than here in Babelsberg. If she hadn't worn gloves, her sweaty fingers would probably have slipped off the sluggish doorknob. Did they have to make the setting so real that they dispensed with handles inside as well? With some effort she opened the door.

The moment "Susan" left the store, Manolo Rioja came out of the dispatch office. "Susan" stopped abruptly and stared at him with her mouth open. Did he see her?

"What's the matter, girl?" shouted Jack Harten impatiently.

"Susan" looked at him, then her gaze landed on Rioja again. She closed her mouth and walked down the two steps to the street as planned. At the same time, she was supposed to look for her cowboy, but her gaze was fixed on Rioja.

"Stop! The whole thing again!" Jack waved both hands and pointed her back into the store.

Sighing, she turned around and went inside.

"Susan" left the store again. Rioja had disappeared. She went down the stairs and looked around for him. Where might he have gone? To the canteen perhaps? Frustrated she frowned.

"Very nice, girl! That's exactly the right expression on your face. – Go on!"

Confused, she blinked at Jack. Then she understood what she was supposed to do.

"Susan" shoved her left fist into her right palm; then she gathered her skirts and strode towards the saloon.

"So far. – Camera!" Jack grinned at "Susan". "Just don't forget your face!"

Carola on the bench across the street giggled from behind her hands. Sometimes she could strangle her.

Even though they were shooting outside, spotlights were switched on to ensure the correct illumination. The cameraman positioned himself; Helen, the script supervisor, stepped forward with the clapperboard.

"Susan" returned to the store.

"Susan" went outside again and looked around searching. Then she made the prescribed steps down the stairs and continued looking around. Still no trace of Rioja. Her shoulders slumped.

Across the street Carola waved her arms wildly and made faces. But what did she have?

Jack had the camera stopped. "All right, again."

"Susan" looked crestfallen.

He came to her and patted her on the back. "No problem, gal. You are still completely new, aren't you? What's your name actually?

"Susan ... uh, Tanja ..." She was thoroughly confused.

"Well, Tanja. Imagine your boyfriend has stood you up. The subway is on strike and you now have to walk home. How would you feel then?"

She narrowed her eyes to slits. "Well, I would tell him

something!" She put her fists on her hips. "Jilt him." Not true at all: She could forgive Micky anything - only she would never get into that situation.

"Exactly! And with that thought you walk into the saloon – to fire Gary."

Relieved she burst out laughing. "I will ponder some murderous thoughts."

Nevertheless it still took a while, but finally the scene was shot. Next, the fight in the saloon was scheduled. It would take half an hour until the location was properly lit. That was also, where Carola had her first appearance; would she still be smirking like that afterwards?

Tanja took off her clammy gloves. "I need a coffee now! If we hurry, we'll make it there and back."

Carola pointed to two men riding leisurely past them. "Next time I'll take my bike with me."

"Good idea; we take the city train. It's not far from Griebnitzsee station to here anyway."

A good distance away from the Western Town they found a self-service cafeteria.

When Tanja opened the door, she gasped in surprise and had to remember to close her mouth. Manolo Rioja sat at the window, in the furthest corner, studying his cell.

She looked nervously at the clock above the counter. It had taken them almost ten minutes to get here and a queue of five people was at the coffee machine.

Carola walked past the waiting people directly to the vending machine. "We have to be right back on the set. I wonder if you could spare us the wait." She put on her best smile and fluttered her eyelashes as she looked at the man next in line. As for the flirting, she was a great actress. In that sense, she probably wouldn't have any trouble with her role as "Daisy".

The man raised his shoulders. "Well..." He turned to the others. "If you don't mind, we'll let them have their coffees."

"Thank you very much." Carola lifted her skirt high enough to show her ankles; then she curtsied in keeping with the times. "Yes, in the Wild West men knew how to treat a lady." She also gave the next one a flirtatious look.

The young man laughed. "We can still do that. Give me the opportunity and I'll prove it."

While Carola continued flirting, Tanja got in front of the vending machine and had it produce two large cappuccinos. She handed Carola a cup, looked around as if she were searching for a place, and then walked straight towards the table where Rioja was sitting.

She put her cup down and thrust out her hand. "I have a scene with you tomorrow," she said in English. "My name is Tanja - in real life." She smiled at him.

He nodded. "I remember you; we were dancing together."

Without asking, she sat opposite him. "I have seen all your movies, Señor Rioja. Even the ones you shot for Spanish television."

"Then I guess I can consider you my fan." He leaned over to the next table and took a paper napkin from the stand there. Then he took a ballpoint pen out of his cell phone purse. "What's your last name?"

She stared at him again and struggled to close her mouth. What would he think of her? He had to take her for an immature teenager if she continued to behave so stupidly.

"Walters," Carola said in her back. "Tanja Walters."

Manolo looked up at her. "Thank you. Are you my fan too?"

Carola cleared her throat and made an embarrassed face.

He grinned. "I can understand that. I, too, find myself quite... *loco*".

Carola laughed, went around the table and sat next to him. As she reached for the sugar sachets in the middle of the table, her hand grazed Manolo's arm – what was that about?

But he unfolded the napkin, unmoved, and began to write.

In between he looked up and glanced at Tanja. She became very hot. What eyes this man had! An abyss in which she could lose herself.

"Exciting." She had whispered, more thinking loudly than wanting to say anything. But Carola raised her eyebrows and made a worried face.

Manolo finished his work with a sweeping signature and pushed the napkin over the table to her. "Tanja?"

She stuttered a few words of thanks before reaching for it. Every word she read made her hotter. With a hoarse voice she thanked him again.

Carola's eyebrows were moving higher and higher and she took the napkin away from Tanja to read the text as well. "I could write you a sample or two for your German fans." She carefully picked up her English. "Not everyone is fit in English." Damn, she could have come up with that herself!

He looked at Carola for a moment, as if he first had to unravel the meaning of her words; then he shook his head. "I have a German teacher for the time I'm shooting here. He does that."

Because of four weeks in Berlin he took the trouble to learn German? Tanja was deeply impressed. "What you start, you do thoroughly, so it seems to me."

He nodded. "The secret to success."

Carola smiled. "That explains a lot."

Manolo looked at her with great interest. Under the

table Tanja kicked Carola against the shin. Why did she have to attract his attention so much? She deprived him of every opportunity to get to know herself.

Carola drank her cappuccino. "We've gotten hired as extra girls. Our break is over." She stood and Tanja had no choice but to follow her.

When she turned around at the door, her gaze crossed that of Manolo. That he looked after her – interesting. Maybe she had made an impression – and hopefully a good one.

Carola bumped her in the side. "Hey, don't fall for him! He's here for four weeks. Then you will never see him again."

Tanja wrinkled her nose. "Who knows. Do you think I could have imagined not only seeing him live, but also getting to know him properly?" She spread her arms and spun one time in a circle. "Everything is possible!

Carola snorted outraged. "He's a movie star!"

"So what? Four weeks are time too."

"And after that?"

She smiled. "Then I have something to remember. Or to tell my grandchildren."

Carola snorted yet again. "You're crazy. *Loco* or whatever."

"Just let me have the fun." She linked arms with her. Now it was really time to go back to shooting.

"And Micky?"

"Micky?" For a moment she didn't have an answer. "It has nothing to do with Micky. And it's none of his business either."

Carola looked even more than before like she thought she was nuts.

5

The first day of shooting was scheduled for a Saturday because of the working square dancers. This time Tanja and Axel were riding with city train and bicycle. The weather was far too nice to torture themselves down the *Avus* as part of the weekend's bumper to bumper traffic. That's what Tanja had told Micky as well when he offered to pick up Axel and her. But most of all she wanted to come and go as it pleased her.

The square dancers' scene was part of a long and highly dramatic sequence: a festival in Los Alamos, despite the war with the Mexicans. While the cannons of battle rumble in the distance, accompanied by fiddle and concertina, the Indians, allied with the Mexicans, sneak up and attack the town. The festival ends in blood and fire. Among the square dancers of the Lietzensee Dance Club, Lydia, Norbert, Chris and Tanja were destined to be corpses.

The beautiful petticoats, in which they usually appeared, were of course not contemporary. That's why they had brought the square dance costumes with the long skirts to the Tuesday rehearsal; but even these had been completely rejected by the outfitter. Also the men's clothes she had discarded as not in proper style: too modern in cut. The costumes she brought to the female dancers that morning were less colorful and consisted of relatively coarse linen and cotton. At least the blouses had some lace. It was hard to believe that the women in Los Alamos did not dress prettier for a festivity.

"We claim to be cultivating the traditions, and then something like that!" Carola watched in the mirror how the hairdresser artfully put up her hair and then pulled out and curled several strands. "But that doesn't seem to me authentic either. Certainly no woman in the Wild West took the time for such an effort. Alone until the curling tongs were hot! A bun and done."

The hairdresser laughed. "Clothes cost money, which the women often did not have. The long hair however..."

"Or a few colorful ribbons." Tanja took a blue velvet ribbon from her dressing table and held it in front of Carola's nose. "How do you hide Madeline's red strand? Spraying over?"

Madeline waved a Quaker's hat, like the one Grace Kelly wore in "High Noon". "It mustn't fall off my head." But there was probably no danger: The hat had wide ribbons with which it was tied at the side of the chin.

When Tanja then arrived outside with Carola and Madeline, Manolo was pacing the scene with Chris. On the sidewalk next to them, the fiddler sat and was writing around in his score with a pencil.

Manolo was dressed in the style of a rich Mexican *haciendero*: black suit, bow tie with long hanging ends and a white frill shirt. No weapon. As a Spaniard he was also visually perfect for his role: The *haciendero* stands between the two sides in this war and stays out for a long time. But the attack on Los Alamos would make him realize that he has to make a choice.

Jack was giving instructions to a young woman who was chalking marks for a tech rehearsal. His smile became wider when his gaze fell on Tanja. "Your hairstyle is certainly Carola's work again."

Carola looked down and knotted her fingers.

Tanja grinned. "She's always been doing the hair of our whole group."

He pointed to the middle of the street. "Chris knows where to line up before the dance begins." Then he went to the pastor's wife of Los Alamos.

Madeline's eyes lit up, as always, even when Chris was simply mentioned by someone. She went to the dance floor.

Carola stopped Tanja when she wanted to follow her. "I'm sure you won't make me popular if you tell everyone I'm doing your hair."

"You think I would offend the hairdressers?" She shrugged. "If you can do it just as well! The poor girls have so much to do; they can be glad you are taking a part of the work off their hands." And Carola should be happy that she put her in the limelight. Hadn't she noticed what chance she had here? She was just too shy; but why? She was good!

Chris reached out to Madeline and pulled her towards him. Then he kissed her as if they hadn't seen each other for a week.

Chris busy; that was her opportunity! Tanja linked arms with Manolo. "Chris is supposed to explain, what we have to do. But now he's busy..." She displayed a mischievous dimple and asked him to show her instead of Chris what to do.

A thousand little wrinkles formed around Manolo's eyes as he returned her smile. He turned to Carola and waved her closer. "I'll explain it to you. "

Tanja raised her eyebrows in warning. Carola did her the favor to keep a straight face and stayed half a step behind as they went to the sidewalk.

Micky left the dressing room together with Norbert. As they walked along the Main Street of Los Alamos, Kincaid came from a side street with a man of the movie fire brigade. Two fire engines stood at its end. Actually something had to burn when the Indians set the city on fire in the afternoon. Then someone had to watch that the fire didn't get out of hand.

Tanja's unmistakable laughter sounded across the street. She was hanging on Rioja's arm and stared at him like a moonstruck calf. Micky clenched his fists. Like Tanja and Carola, he should have gotten himself an extra role; one in which he could fight – preferably with Rioja.

The musician sat with dangling legs on the sidewalk and tuned his violin... or fiddle... or whatever he was playing. Jack Harten and his script supervisor were discussing with two men in shorts and t-shirts. According to their clothes, they probably belonged to the technical staff and were able to make their lives bearable. This morning there was no sand dust blowing along the road. It was windless and already oppressively hot. Micky tugged impatiently at his shirt collar; he would rather have rolled up his sleeves.

Nobert whistled appreciatively as they approached the group around Rioja. "Our girls! Chic!" He nodded a greeting to Rioja and Tanja and gave Carola a kiss on the cheek before linking arms with her and then also greeting Madeline.

Micky squinted his eyes in anger as his gaze wandered back and forth between Tanja and Rioja. Why did he hold her so intimately? "What are we waiting for?"

"We get paid per day. Who cares what we do in that time?" Carola pointed with a movement of her head to Jack, who had just been taken over by Kincaid. "They'll know..."

A lighting tech came to them. "Manolo, where are you going to be on the dance floor?" His English was perfect. Probably that was a prerequisite for everyone who was hired here.

Rioja withdrew his arm from Tanja and followed the man up the stairs.

"What are you doing?" Micky hissed at her when Rioja was out of earshot.

"What are you talking about?"

He snorted indignantly. "About you throwing yourself at Rioja."

"Micky, what do you think of her?" Carola rammed her hands into her hips.

Madeline chuckled. "Wait until rehearsal. Then you can put yourself unrestrained in scene." She pulled Micky away from Tanja. "Calm down. We're here to have fun and make a few bucks for the club."

"Fun!" Micky's face began to blaze with anger. "That's no fun anymore!" He ripped the Stetson from his head and fired it against the railing of the sidewalk. Slowly the hat sailed onto the road. To his greatest satisfaction, he instantly fell under the hooves of a horse.

Chris turned to them, a question mark on his face. He had obviously noticed that something was going on. "What's the matter with you all of a sudden?"

Micky glared at him and snorted outraged. Chris better kept an eye on the girls.

"Get yourself a new hat from the pool. You can probably forget this one now."

Micky snorted again. "I don't need a new hat." He straightened his shoulders and stomped away.

"Micky!"

Determined, he ignored Chris' shout. He was done with the circus here.

Stunned, Tanja stared after Micky. What was he thinking, getting all puffed up like that?

Chris turned to Madeline. "What happened?"

"Just a moment!" She pushed Tanja. "Get him back." Like Micky would care what she said.

"I'll handle this," Carola said quickly and ran off.

Norbert hesitated for a moment, then he followed her.

"They won't achieve anything." Madeline pressed her lips together, exasperated. "Tanja, it's up to you to talk some sense into him!"

She stomped her foot. "It's not my fault if Micky makes a mess of the shooting." Madeline looked at her as if she disagreed.

Manolo jumped off the dance floor and came to them. "Let's start!" He nodded invitingly to Chris and Jack.

"Everybody leave the scene." All those who had nothing to do on the scene stepped behind the cameras.

Chris looked back at the end of the street where the three missing square dancers had disappeared. A steep furrow stood between his eyebrows as he looked again at Tanja. "Line-up!"

They climbed the five steps to the dance floor. Tanja blatantly blocked Bettina's path and stood next to Manolo. Bettina looked at her bewildered and then made do with Axel.

"Who's missing?" Helen pointed to the gap in Madeline's square.

"No problem." Chris hesitated for a moment. "We'll do the first rehearsal without the three."

"Three?" Helen sounded shocked. She turned her head looking back and forth. "What are they doing?

"They'll be right back!" Chris' voice didn't waver, but the furrow on his forehead showed his concern. Nevertheless, he gave the fiddler the cue, put his hands on his hips and started his calls after the first bars.

"... half sashay." Tanja let go of Manolo's hand and sashayed so close in front of him to his other side that she grazed him with her skirt. This morning she had used a heavy exotic perfume. "... swing your girl." She held her head as close to his face as inconspicuously possible. Tanja was only a few inches smaller than Manolo and his breath caressed her forehead. After the spin he could have kissed her, but he apparently didn't want to. After all, the script gave him some freedom. She really couldn't show herself more inviting without the others noticing.

Carola and Norbert came around the street corner. They began to run; shortly after they stood in front of the dance floor, panting. Norbert stretched out his hands in a helpless gesture. "Micky's gone!"

"Darn!" Chris squinted his eyes angrily. "Come up. We repeat whilst I think." But of course there wasn't much to think about; to save the shooting day they needed a replacement for Micky on the spot.

Had it not been for the gap in the square, the rehearsal would have been perfect. Madeline seemed close to tears as Chris descended the dance floor after the repeat to tell Jack that they were missing a dancer.

"Why didn't you say so straight away?" For now, Jack seemed more bewildered than angry.

"Because Mr. Hassloff was still here twenty minutes ago." Twenty minutes already? Micky really should come back now; meanwhile he had to have calmed down.

Jack rubbed his chin. "What happened?"

"I don't know exactly." Chris raised his shoulders. That might still pass as truth. "He got sick." Well, that was true somehow, too. "That's why he couldn't stay." Chris had managed without an open lie; but would it do any good?

"Do we have a replacement?," Jack asked his script supervisor.

Helen shook her head.

Thereupon he turned to Chris again. "Do we have a replacement?"

Chris pulled his cell out and leafed through the directory.

Jack watched him with obviously growing displeasure. "How long will it take you to get someone here?"

Chris' answer was too quiet to understand it up on the dance floor. Jack went a few steps aside with Helen and seemed to be discussing with her. Chris chewed on his lower lip; then he pressed a number on his cell.

Madeline gave Tanja an angry look. "You got us into this with your flirting," she hissed, "Do you have any idea what it will cost the club if the contract blows up?"

Tanja shrugged; what could happen? Surely Chris knew someone in another club who was willing to step in. But his face was darkening more and more while he was on the phone. Maybe she should have tried to stop Micky after all. But what the hell did he have to behave like an idiot? It was just childish to begrudge her flirting with Manolo.

Jack came to the edge of the dance floor and turned to the dancers. "We have another solution for the moment. For you the shooting day is over. Next Saturday at eight please be back here. Everybody!"

Manolo jumped off the dance floor with a long Spanish curse and went to the dispatch office.

Madeline slowly blew the air out of her mouth. "By then Micky will hopefully have calmed down. Or will he?"

Norbert patted her on the back. "Micky isn't one to let us down."

"Today he did!" Tanja gave an angry growl.

Madeline stared at her as if she had something to say about it. But then she just sighed and climbed down to Chris.

"Let's pack it up, guys." Chris put his cell away.

Tanja went into the dressing room ahead of the others and changed silently. When she stepped outside again, Manolo was standing with a furious Kincaid in front of Chris and Jack. Kincaid was loud, but his English had such a heavy slang that she understood virtually nothing.

Chris looked angry now, too.

Madeline came out of the door behind her and stopped. "I'm waiting for Chris."

Carola slipped past Madeline and linked arms with Tanja. But she hardly noticed it. With her gaze she followed Manolo who went to the saloon. He hadn't looked at her at all after the rehearsal had ended.

He stopped behind the swinging door. A black-haired beauty approached him so quickly that she must have waited for him. Tanned shoulders above the hem of a strapless bright red top. The rest of her physique was concealed by the swing door; it was most certainly breathtaking. With her feet slightly open, she stood before him in flat silver sandals and laid her hands on his shoulders.

"She looks like another star," Carola remarked dryly.

"If so, what?" Manolo was constantly harassed by some women who wanted to be seen with him. But so far none of them had managed to get on a picture with him more than twice. "Probably one of those groupies! Do you think I don't stand a chance against them?"

"But Tanja!" Carola sounded shocked. "As a groupie?"

Tanja started moving towards the saloon and tried to pull Carola with her.

"Where are you going?" Carola freed herself from her.

"I thought we wanted to leave?" She shrugged, then she went on alone.

But before she reached the saloon, Manolo and the black-haired woman disappeared from her field of vision.

Now there was no longer an inconspicuous approach. She growled in frustration.

The next moment Carola was again standing next to her. "We have more important things to do. Make sure you reach Micky and bring him to his senses."

Why did they all blame her for the chaos Micky had caused? Tanja swung her backpack over her shoulder and got her bike. Then she made her way to the city train without waiting for Axel.

She wouldn't call Micky for sure – after all, what could she tell him? Should she beg maybe? Or lie to him to appease him?

6

When Micky entered the Lietzensee Dance Club on Tuesday afternoon, George Lagrange was standing wide-legged at the door to the office. He hadn't expected him; never before he had been so early on a Tuesday. But actually it didn't matter; whether it was just Chris wringing his neck or George as well... Anyway, it had been a stupid idea to come to practice today. But he wasn't one to skive off.

Almost the whole group was already there. Tanja was missing – still? And when she came, what then? Maybe he should forego practicing altogether until the whole circus with the shooting was over. For once they would get along without him.

Madeline slipped off her bar stool and raised an arm. "Micky, here we are." As if he hadn't seen that. Probably she didn't know what to say either. Chris was already standing there too, an empty glass in his hand.

The chatter of the square dancers abruptly stopped; one by one they looked at him expectantly.

Micky smiled for a moment at Madeline's zeal. Then he grimly pressed his lips together and looked at George. "I have no appointment with you, George."

George actually let him go to the bar without comment; but he followed. Micky tried to ignore him.

"If our troupe wasn't so important to me, I wouldn't have come at all, Chris." He pulled up a bar stool and leaned with one elbow on the seat.

Marga Fischer, behind the counter, held a bottle of beer to him, questioning. Did the office assistant always have to play the big carer? He didn't want beer now.

"But?" Madeline seemed to be struggling not to hiss at him. "When someone starts like that, there's always a 'but'."

George stopped a few steps away, clearly tense. "You want to have square dancing in our club? And ruin your and our reputation?"

Micky snorted. "Who will ruin our reputation more? A dancer who is indisposed, or a dancer who behaves like a groupie?"

Madeline raised her hand. "Micky, that was an insult." The warning undertone in her voice was unmistakable. "If such behavior gains ground among us, the group will quickly fall apart."

Suddenly he had a sinking feeling in his stomach. If someone told Tanja, what would she think of him? "I... I cherish Tanja. I would never want to insult her."

"Then why do you do it?" Chris asked. "What do you think you can achieve with your childish behavior?"

That Tanja came to her senses. Micky shrugged; it was pointless to answer a provocative question.

"The club has signed a contract." George gritted his teeth. "You answer to me that we're complying with it."

Micky spun around angrily. "Are you threatening me, George? You can't threaten me. Go to the devil!"

"Do you think I can't do that?" George's face was flushing. "I'll kick you out of the club if you don't show up in Babelsberg on Saturday." Angrily he narrowed his eyes to slits . "And you stay and do your job. You have taken on an obligation!"

"Did I? Well, so what! As far as I'm concerned, the whole club can go to hell with you. As if there was nothing more important in the world!" But without the club he wouldn't see Tanja anymore; Micky quelled a sigh. His gaze went to Chris. "I'm sorry," he said in a softer voice. Then he pushed his shoulders back, turned around and went to the exit. He would miss them all.

"That means damaging the club," George yelled after him. In a moment he would spit fire. "I will ruin you!"

Tanja stood in front of the drawing board in her apartment and pressed her hands at her lower abdomen. She hadn't had such bad cramps in years. She might have to call Chris and cancel practice. Anyway, a woman shouldn't do sports during those days. On the other hand... She had never canceled for this reason; he probably wouldn't believe her.

After a look at the clock she went to the bathroom and took a painkiller. It was supposed to work in time for her to endure the square dance afternoon. After all, she also wanted to know if Chris had found a replacement for Saturday. Or if someone had managed to bring Micky to his senses.

She boiled a chamomile tea to calm her stomach, because she was sick too. With her tea she then nibbled listlessly on a rusk; immediately afterwards she regurgitated both. Actually, she was really sick. But nobody would believe her this apology; not after the scandal on Saturday. And how would she look then?

When she brushed her teeth to get rid of the disgusting taste, the mirror showed her a corpse. Hideous! She reached deep into the clay potty with the African Earth and in return skipped the black eyeliner before setting off.

Of course the bus got stuck in a traffic jam and the subway drove away right under her nose. When she got off, it was exactly five to half past five. She hurried up the escalator to the street, ignoring the tearing pain in her belly, and set off on a trot.

She stopped in the courtyard's driveway to the dance club and drew breath. Micky's motorcycle stood next to the stairway to the floor. She exhaled with a sigh of relief. That was certainly a good omen for Saturday. Norbert was obviously right: Micky wasn't one to let the group down.

She wiped her forehead with the back of her hand, smoothed her hair and steeled herself for the encounter with him. Hopefully she didn't have to tell him first that Manolo was nothing more than some prince charming.

As she walked past Micky's motorcycle, she gently brushed across the seat; the black leather had absorbed the warmth of the sun. Riding a motorcycle looked cool. She could tell Micky that she would like to roar with him down the *Avus* for once, leaning against his back and wrapping her arms around his waist. No, certainly she couldn't say it like that. Simply: "Micky, can I ride with you sometime? I've never sat on a motorcycle before." But maybe he didn't have a second helmet and she would embarrass him. Maybe that's why he always came by car when he picked her up. She better not ask him at all.

Still looking at the bike, she opened the door to the stairwell. A few floors above her, a door crashed into the lock; then someone ran down the stairs.

Micky! He had torn his hair out and his gaze was gloomy. What had happened?

Abruptly he stopped on the landing above her. "Tanja!"

"Hi Micky!" She tried to hide her bewilderment behind a smile. "Where are you going?"

"None of your business." More slowly he walked down the stairs. He was upset; about what now?

As he was going to pass her, she grabbed his arm. "But

what happened? Don't we have any practice today?" Silly question; Chris would have told everyone off in time. But somehow she had to make him talk.

"You do!" Micky actually stopped. "But I have no practice today. Maybe never again."

What was that supposed to mean? Tanja was speechless for a moment. "Just like that? You just drop everything?" Anger rose in her as Micky shrugged at that and shoved her hand away. "How can you do something like that?"

"As if square dancing was important for anything!"

"Isn't it?"

He bit his lips and shook his head. Somehow he didn't look happy at all – as if he wasn't sure of his decision. "I have to take care of the university. Getting my new program to work." He justified himself; how nice! Maybe she could get him to stay.

"Now during the semester break?" With a laugh she let him hear her mockery. "I didn't know you needed that!"

He glared at her angrily, but this time he didn't fall for the provocation: Instead of picking it up, he simply shrugged again and continued down the stairs. He just walked away?

Tanja only found her tongue when he opened the courtyard door. She put her hands on her hips. "If you think I'm running after you, you're on the wrong track! There are enough dancers who can replace you."

When Micky's motorcycle roared, she burst into tears. She squatted on the stairs and put her head on her knees. Presumably the others had started practicing in the meantime and wondered if she too would let them down. But she couldn't pick herself up; besides, she now didn't have a partner anyway,

Again the door of the floor slammed shut above her. George came down the stairs. The old man was just what she needed that day.

51

"Tanja, have you seen your partner?" he thundered through the stairwell.

Tanja wiped her tears off with her skirt and stood. "What do you want from Micky?"

"I'll kick him out!" George was about to explode.

"Then you may well be pleased that he's gone!" Was that it? Micky hadn't left because of her, but because of George? "What have you done now?" Another argument because he didn't want to have square dancing in the club anyway?

Well, that would just suit him! And he could save his answer as well. Tanja swung her backpack over her shoulder and pushed him aside. She hurried up the stairs to get to practice.

7

Micky parked his motorcycle at the fence in front of the old "Café Einstein" in Tiergarten's Kurfürstenstraße and went up to the bar on the first floor. It was unusually crowded even for a Friday evening; probably some event had just come to an end nearby.

In passing, he ordered a big *Kölsch* at the counter and then sat at one of the round tables on the terrace. The waitress followed him with the beer almost on his heels.

Morose, he stared at it; then at his cell. Where was Carola?

Ten minutes later she stood a little breathless in the doorway, pushed her way through the crowd and dropped onto the chair opposite him with a loud breath. She pointed to the full beer glass. "Did you want to drown your frustration and then realized that the beer doesn't taste good?"

"Ha, ha!" He screwed up his mouth; he really wasn't up for small talk. "What are you up to that the phone isn't good enough for you?"

"Face to face," she fluttered her eyelids, "I can play out all my not inconsiderable charm to talk some sense into you." She called for the waitress who had just come into view.

Micky grabbed his beer and drank a long sip. Then he screwed up his mouth again. "Turned stale." He looked her in the eye as he put the glass down. "Like so many things."

Visibly startled, Carola reached for his hand. "Does

that mean you'll really stop dancing?" He had actually been able to provoke her; why didn't that work for Tanja?

"And if so?"

"But Micky!"

The waitress reached their table, balancing a tray of empty glasses. "What can I get you?"

"A cherry juice." Carola seemed to delight in her bewildered face. The bar was renowned for its great cocktails; non-alcoholic was rarely in demand. "Don't you have any?"

"Yes, we do."

"I'd like a new beer." He pushed his glass to the waitress. "I had to wait too long for company."

The waitress nodded and placed the glass on her tray. "Coming right up!"

Carola's gaze followed her for a moment, then she turned back to him. "You are not serious that you want to quit. You're just saying to annoy me."

He smiled bitterly. "I could upset you with that?" If only Tanja wasn't indifferent about it. But she hadn't moved from the spot when he had walked away from the shooting.

Carola sighed. "Micky, we are your friends. Don't let us down! We don't deserve that."

"That playboy! I'm not going to let that prick take my girl from me." Angrily he pressed his lips together.

"Tanja's not your girl, Micky. She doesn't even know that you love her! You never told her."

"It's a natural guess."

"Oh really?" Carola wiggled her eyebrows; she suddenly seemed to be enjoying herself.

"If she loved me, she would sense it without me having to say anything."

"Aha!" She grinned almost gloatingly.

He looked at her, uncomprehending. What did she mean by that?

"And what about you?"

He understood less and less what she was aiming for.

Carola was now smirking completely unabashed. "If one notices something like that – why haven't you noticed how Tanja feels about you?

He stared at the table.

"Why don't you dare go after her when you should know she has fallen in love as well?

He looked up, unsure what to answer. "She never..."

"...said a word." Carola burst out laughing. "Neither did you! What a pair of kids you both are!"

The waitress came and hastily put their drinks in front of them.

"Thank you." Carola put on a smile for her, but she was already on her way to the next table.

"Then why does she let this bloke ensnare her?"

"Oh, all girls have some flame they hang as poster over their beds at home." She turned bright red. "I've got one of those things on the wall, too."

But what kind of argument was that? He reached for his glass and emptied it halfway. "That's better." With the back of his hand he wiped the foam off his mouth. "But your teenage crushes aren't real. This one is." He pressed his lips angrily together and breathed heavily. "I can't compete with what he promises her. She doesn't even see that he's lying to her."

"He doesn't, Micky. He doesn't dream of promising her anything, let alone lying to her."

"How do you know that? You don't even know him."

"But you do, Micky?" Her gaze wandered through the room as if she was searching for something. She seemed to get nervous. "I have talked to him."

She drank a sip of her cherry juice and licked her lips with relish. "Markedly good. Real juice, no lemonade. Maybe I should eat something?" She turned around for the waitress. But suddenly she reached over the table for his hand. "Look, a woman from the set."

Her arms protectively in front of her, a black-haired woman in a tentlike cut, wide falling dress slowly moved towards the counter and seemed to look for a vacancy.

He scrutinized the woman's face. "I can't remember. In our scene she is definitely not present."

Carola rose halfway and waved in her direction. The woman reacted with a smile and then approached them.

Carola sat again. "Go get Consuela a chair."

"Consuela?" He was completely flabbergasted. The extra part had apparently made Carola keen on filming. "I thought you wanted to talk to me about Tanja."

She shrugged resignedly. "I don't know what else to say to convince you." Carola gave in? That could not be. Suspiciously he narrowed his eyes.

The woman she had called Consuela was standing in front of them. Stunned, he stared for a moment at the clearly bulging belly that he had at eye level in front of him. From the distance and in the crowd around the counter, the robe had completely concealed her pregnancy.

He got a hold of himself and stood. "I'll get you a chair!"

Consuela said something that sounded like English but he nevertheless didn't understand.

When he came back to the table with a chair, Carola pointed at him and collected her English. "This is Micky Hasloff from our square dance group."

He positioned the chair for Consuela.

A thin smile appeared in the corners of her mouth. "The one, who blew the scene last Saturday."

That he did understand. His face began to blaze and he lowered his gaze. "I had my reasons!" He would have loved to blow up more than just the scene. Defiantly he pressed his teeth onto his lower lip and sat again. "What role do you play in the movie?" He tried to keep his gaze on Consuela's face.

"None at all." She stroked her belly. "Manolo wants to make sure he can be there at the birth. That's why I came to Berlin during the shooting."

"Manolo?" He frowned.

"Manolo Rioja. Don't you know he's the star of the movie?"

"Yes, I do!" Involuntarily he clenched his fists.

"And the star of my life."

"What?"

Consuela's smile widened and something began to dawn on him.

"Then the child will probably become a Berliner." Carola smiled cheerfully.

"Or Potsdamer. We booked a room in a hospital there, too." Following Carola's gaze, she turned around.

Manolo Rioja stood in the entrance to the bar. In passing he grabbed a free chair and came to them. "I'm sure I'll get a parking ticket. But I've already driven so far that I hardly know if I'll ever find the car again."

Micky turned his beer glass between his hands and looked at him thoughtfully. "Such a coincidence," he murmured in German.

"He will hardly leave her alone in her condition," Carola whispered back.

Rioja put his hand on Consuela's back, said something in Spanish and kissed her on the temple. Then he looked at Micky. "May I sit?"

He already had his chair! Micky snorted angrily; then he

had himself under control again. "I was amazed when Consuela showed up here. Now I'm not surprised anymore."

Rioja nodded. "Right. Our appearance here was planned." He turned his gaze to Carola. "This seemed the best way to prove that I'm not in your way." He caressed Consuela's nape. "And neither am I interested in your beautiful girlfriend."

Underneath the table Micky clenched his fist. "Tanja is not my girlfriend."

"And that's your problem." Consuela settled more comfortably and leaned against Rioja's shoulder. "Movie stars often have a bad reputation and Manolo's manager takes care of his as being a lady's man. That's how showbiz is."

"But in truth, there's nothing to it?" Micky looked at her in disbelief. "I googled!"

"And found all those photos with girls at Manolo's side." Consuela smirked. "They are all models who get paid for their performance." She pointed to Carola. "We also hired Carola yesterday when she was at our hotel. 'Berlin hairdresser Rioja's new love' will be a nice headline."

Carola blushed and stuttered something unintelligible.

"I don't believe it!" If that were true, then he would have made a fool of himself in a grandiose way. No, that was a conspiracy. They just wanted to get him to return to the set. He growled contemptuously.

Rioja shrugged. "We have been married for five years and have two daughters. With this strategy, so far we've been able to keep our marriage out of the headlines."

Carola reached for Micky's hand. "Don't be so stubborn. Can't you see that Consuela would stake her life on her husband's fidelity?"

"Bah! They're both actors, after all!"

Consuela and Rioja listened to their exchange with strained faces; did they understand anything? They should just hear how much he despised them for their transparent maneuver.

Carola smiled briefly at Rioja, then turned back to him. "Micky! They've only been married for five years and obviously are having already their third child!" She breathed so fiercely as if she was about to lose her temper. "That doesn't speak exactly for an unhappy marriage!"

He squirmed uneasily and grabbed his beer. It was already stale again.

"Micky, please come to the shooting tomorrow morning." Rioja wrapped his arm around Consuela. "You would do us a big favor if I could finish my shooting as planned. Our girls shouldn't wait any longer than necessary to meet their new brother."

Carola looked surprised. "Won't you have them brought to Berlin?"

"We didn't find a suitable house that we could rent for the short time. Otherwise we would have taken them with us anyway."

Consuela nodded. "As long as the children don't go to school, we try not to let them suffer from our profession."

"Then you are really an actress too? But you're not as well known as your husband." As if he had known Rioja before. Tanja had never told him anything about her crush. Otherwise he would have prevented the group from accepting the movie contract.

"I work first and foremost in the theater. And I sing."

"Micky, what can I do to convince you? We have this joint scene with square dancing; there's nothing we can do about it."

"And Tanja has two more scenes with you. I read the part she plays."

Carola rolled her eyes. "Maybe you'll stop just standing

there mute and angry? Maybe you will tell her what you want from her?"

"What if she turns me down again?"

"Again!" Carola gasped. "When and where did she turn you down? I'd know that!"

"On Tuesday before practice."

She frowned. "She told you she didn't love you?"

Micky growled. "She treated me totally offhand."

"I just don't believe that! Not Tanja; it's not like her." She shook her head. "Unless, of course, she was terribly angry."

He grimaced. "Well, of course she was!"

Rioja and Consuela got more and more question marks in their eyes. Carola began to summarize what they had just talked about. How embarrassing! Micky put a hand on her arm to slow her down. That would be the last straw that Carola told them everything down to the last detail. They already had to think he was an idiot anyway.

Then he turned to Rioja himself. "I'll come to the shooting tomorrow morning. You can't help Tanja's insanity. So it wouldn't be fair to make you suffer from it." His gaze went to Consuela's belly, which forced her to sit a bit away from the table. "In your condition, of all things."

Relief was spreading across Rioja's face. He waved at the waitress. "Bring us a glass of mineral water and a bottle of champagne with four glasses," he ordered in English.

As the drinks were standing on the table, Micky raised his glass to the tiny sip in Consuela's glass. "As long as our group is busy shooting, you don't have to worry. Our caller is a paramedic with the fire brigade in his real profession. Presumably Chris has already helped more than one child into the world, who didn't want to wait for the trip to the hospital."

Carola laughed out loud. "That would be an experience."

Rioja grinned. "We could suggest Kincaid an addition to the script. With an extra part for Chris."

Micky took the cell out of his pocket and started to scroll through the list of names.

"What are you up to?" Maybe for the sake of the two of them Carola stayed with English.

Now that question perplexed him after all. "Shouldn't we tell Chris?"

"That he has got one more job?" Consuela grabbed her mineral water with a half-suppressed giggle.

"Will you call George, too?"

Micky swallowed; then he nodded valiantly. "I guess I have no choice but to fix what I've wrecked."

Then he told Chris straight away that he would be punctually in Babelsberg in the morning. "I tell George myself," he concluded the conversation with a sigh.

Chris laughed quietly. "You don't have to do that to yourself. I'm with Madeline and he's sitting in the kitchen. Anyway, as far as he's able to sit still."

"Chris, you are the best. Thank you."

"But Tanja is no longer here. She's the one you should call."

"No!" That sounded too dismissive. He closed his eyes, then exhaled slowly. "Did she condition it on my coming whether she goes to Babelsberg tomorrow morning? Or what?"

"Not that I know of." In the background, Madeline's voice came through the phone. Chris seemed to hold his hand to his cell, because he received only muffled and incomprehensible, which was probably his answer for Madeline. Then Chris was back with him. "Micky, you don't have to justify anything to me. I'm glad you're coming tomorrow." He told him briefly how much of the scene they had rehearsed before they had to stop.

After another half minute Micky closed his cell and exhaled with relief.

8

Tanja was tired out. Even more than the heavy thunderstorm the nightmare had kept her awake, Micky would be chucking the shooting. What if Chris hadn't gotten him to see reason?

Before taking a shower, she put her cell on the bathroom console. All she had to do was reach out when he called. But Micky didn't call. Maybe it was better that way: He would laugh at her if she told him that he had no reason for jealousy because he was more important to her than any movie star in the world.

Still, she continued to sneak around the phone before breakfast. She could ask him to pick her up because there were still heavy rain clouds in the sky. To arrive soaking wet in Babelsberg was not an option. But she could not come to a decision.

As she poured her second coffee, Lydia Aydemir unexpectedly rang at her front door. Now she didn't have to give herself away – but she didn't know either whether Micky would come.

.Sakir leaned against the driver's door and grinned at her. Lydia was to be envied for her husband: Unmusical like a poker, he still supported her enthusiastically. She would like to have a guy like that one day. Not musically challenged. One who supported her unconditionally.

He opened the car door for Tanja. "Lydia threw up her breakfast because of stage fright. Can you imagine that?"

No, she couldn't. She stared at Lydia. "Certainly not because of the scene. She just has to dance as usual." She wiped her wet palms against each other. "Certainly not."

Now Lydia was even blushing. What a sight! Tanja shook her head in amazement as she got in.

In the dressing room Carola stood with a hairdresser behind another background actor; together they were working the woman's corkscrew curls. Carola reacted with a chuckle to a remark of the hairdresser. She looked just as relaxed when she did the dancers' hair in the club. Obviously it were indeed the conditions at the salon that made her miserable with her job.

Madeline entered the dressing room, greeted Carola and Lydia with a kiss, patted Tanja on the back and greeted the other square dancers with a wave. "All set, gals?" She sat and took off her sandals. "Have all our people gathered in the meantime? Do you happen to know that?"

Tanja exhaled slowly to control her rising anger. "Why don't you say right away you want to know whether Micky has come! And no, I didn't look to see if he's already here." She pointed to Madeline's cell on the dressing table. "Chris can tell you." But Chris would certainly have called her if Micky hadn't come. Why did Madeline really ask?

"Micky always comes at the last minute. Or after that." Carola giggled. "I've never seen him wasting even five minutes."

Lydia laughed. The two of them had certainly had no nightmares.

Tanja bit her lips so as not to burst out. What did they all want from her? She turned her back on them and took her costume off the clothes rail.

In the end, she was one of the last to be finished with her hair and make-up. Carola was still left to go; she had worked hand in hand with one of the hairdressers all the time.

Together with Madeline Tanja left the dressing room. It was located at the back of the studio building; those for the stars were more centrally placed. Maybe she ran into Manolo; she knew exactly which one was his dressing room. Leisurely she strolled after Madeline.

Eventually Madeline linked arms with her and forced her to take a faster step. "Do you miss... something?

"Shouldn't we wait for Carola?"

Madeline laughed. "Carola is the least of my concerns." She looked at her wristwatch. "Oh damn it! I forgot to take it off!"

Madeline's being distracted for a moment was just what she needed. She freed herself from her arm and stopped. She was in no hurry to get outside. Not yet.

A few doors ahead of them Manolo came out of his dressing room. The black-haired girl from the saloon leaned into the door frame. Tanja's mouth fell open: The woman was pregnant, unmissable. Manolo put his arm around her and kissed her on the forehead.

Tanja closed her mouth again and snorted indignantly.

Madeline turned around and grabbed her arm. "This must be Consuela."

Tanja blinked in confusion. "Consuela?"

Madeline laughed. "You read everything about Rioja you can get your hands on and don't even know he's married? And happily, apparently."

Tanja suddenly had a lump in her throat. "How do you know she's his wife?"

"Carola met her. And she described her to us."

"Us?"

Madeline shrugged. "We sat together last night – Chris, Grandpa and I. We were like cats on hot bricks, waiting whether Carola manages to move Micky to get here."

Tanja kept staring at the couple in front of them. Manolo stroked the woman's neck. "Have you conspired against me?"

"Why against you? Wasn't Micky our problem?"

Tanja blinked to fight down the tears that threatened in her eyes. Then she walked with giant steps towards the exit of the building. As she passed Manolo, she turned her head away.

Only when she opened the door to the outside did the staccato of Madeline's boots sound behind her. Outside, Hinnerk intercepted her after a few steps. He seemed to notice that something wasn't right because he stroked her arm wordlessly. With clenched teeth she let him accompany her to the dance floor. Manolo married – that couldn't be. He wasn't the type of guy to play his fans like that.

Madeline came at Manolo's side, her skirts gathered to avoid dragging them through the puddles left by the night's tempest. Manolo had a laughter on his face when she said something to him.

Hinnerk was still holding Tanja's arm. Did he think she would run away like Micky?

"Buenas dias!" Manolo smiled at Tanja. "Good morning, dear fan." He frowned. "Dear fan? Does that work in German?"

Hinnerk answered in English. "You have to take the real German word." He wiggled his nose. "Although there is actually none."

"Devotee," said Madeline. "Paladin. "

"This is from the Middle Ages, my dear." Hinnerk smirked. " We better take straight away... enthusiast... worshipper?"

Madeline's eyes suddenly lit up and she pointed with her head to the studio door. Chris was standing there and

Norbert and Micky walked past him to the outside. Directly afterwards the other square dancers came onto the street and Chris followed them.

Tanja looked to the ground to avoid Micky's gaze. She didn't want to know now, how he looked at her.

Chris put his arm around Madeline's shoulder and kissed her on the tip of her nose. "I have missed you, darling."

"You just haven't seen each other for too long." Grinning, Hinnerk dragged Madeline away from Chris. "But now she belongs to me to begin with." He helped her up the steps to the dance floor.

Chris greeted Manolo. "We don't have to wait for the director to warm up."

Manolo nodded. "I'm very much in favor of saving time."

Carola linked arms with him. What was she thinking? After all, Manolo was in her square. "Everything okay with Consuela?"

"She went back to the dressing room to lay down." He looked around. "Still no paparazzi today who want to catch both of us?"

The two cameramen put their equipment in position and assigned Chris his place at the edge of the dance floor. The fiddler sat on the sidewalk in front of the sheriff's office and began tuning his fiddle string by string. Jack Harten came from the dispatch office with Helen, the script supervisor, a steaming plastic cup at his mouth.

Manolo went to Jack and exchanged a few words with him; then he climbed onto the dance floor. "We have a quarter of an hour before things get serious. By then Josh will have finished tuning, too."

Madeline translated it for those who couldn't follow the English exchange well enough.

For lack of music Chris raised his hand to give the go-ahead for the first rehearsal. Then he let it sink again and looked at Tanja. "Swap places with Lydia." He wanted her to get out of the square with Manolo. Apparently he didn't trust Micky yet. Or her?

Her gaze went to Manolo, who stood opposite and looked so composed that he certainly hadn't understood Chris. She pressed her lips together and made room for Lydia, who had immediately followed Chris' request.

Chris exhaled, visibly relieved. Then he raised his arm again and started his calls. Before they had danced through the figures once, Chris had stopped three times and had them repeated. On this morning Beate and Franz, the two background actors, were very inattentive.

Tanja just wanted to be done with it. None of her expectations had been fulfilled; and now Manolo was even in another square. "It doesn't have to be perfect." During the cut, they would anyway choose which pieces to take. "We're just ordinary people from Los Alamos, not saloon dancers."

"Don't think of any ways to put in mishaps! No arbitrariness today, Tanja." Chris was obviously in a bad mood. What else bothered him? The shooting couldn't be it any more.

Hinnerk grabbed Madeline's hand, looking at Chris from the corner of his eye. "Do you have a fight, you two?"

"Not that I know of."

"Then he's in trouble with George again!" Hinnerk growled. "Your grandfather should finally leave his office to the younger ones."

Madeline just shrugged.

"Is everyone here now?" Jack asked from below.

Helen stood at the edge of the dance floor and counted the dancers with her fingers. "Nobody's missing."

The director gave the fiddler a sign and Josh rose from his place on the sidewalk.

"You dance it now undisturbed one time and this is how we tape it then." He drew his eyebrows together. "Just in case."

They started again, this time with the fiddle. That Chris didn't sing was still unusual and it took Tanja the verve out of her movements. Or was it something else?

Micky seemed completely insouciant and in high spirits. He hadn't had a sleepless night either. Again and again he laughed at Ana, of whom she knew in the meantime that she played the daughter of the *haciendero* and lost her lover in the attack of the Indians.

The instructions Jack gave in the meantime and the movement in front of the dance floor clearly showed that time was getting short. Without further comment, he then let it shoot. After that at least, he made a few contented sounds. Chris ran his sleeve over his forehead; he sweated more than the dancers. Two make-up artists came up to the dance floor and hurriedly repaired their make-ups.

Then Jack stepped to the edge of the dance floor. "Well, here comes the difficult part."

In the last quarter of the scene, the dancers gradually become aware of the attack. Because the Indians only shoot with bows and arrows, there is no noise to warn the town. First Hinnerk, then Carola, accidentally perceive movements, while they look during their spins into a side alley between the houses. They stop short and get out of step. After some quiet exchange, the second square becomes attentive. But they still don't understand that Indians are sneaking around the city. Then the warning cry of a man who is not fatally hit suddenly alerts everyone. Only the fiddler, who is half deaf, continues to play until he finally realizes that nobody is dancing anymore. He apparently made the comic relief in the movie.

Of course, this part of the scene was the more important part of their performance. Ten times they rehearsed only that half-minute from seeing the "movements" on the outskirts of town to the whispers in the first square.

Eventually Jack was satisfied enough for the first take. But they had been mistaken when they thought it was done now. Jack still had a number of change requests and in the end it was lunchtime when they actually had this piece wrapped up.

While the dancers were allowed to leave for lunch, Chris went to the dispatch office with Jack to discuss the time after lunch break.

Micky helped his partner, the "daughter of the *haciendero*", down the steps from the dance floor. Ana had studied at the *"Escuela de Interpretación"* of Cristina Rota in Madrid. Which meant that she too had to be a renowned actress; but this was her first international film.

As she stood on the ground, she first looked around for Manolo Rioja, then turned to Micky. "Will you come to lunch with me?" she asked in her broken English. She would certainly be better off with Rioja, but she didn't seem to expect him to have time for her.

Micky gallantly held out his arm to her. *"¡Sí, Señorita!"* Ana saved him from having to deal with Tanja now. When Chris had given him the position at Ana's side again, it was such a relief.

He had expected Rioja to first check on his wife, but he made his way to the canteen with Lydia. Maybe he met Consuela there.

Tanja hurried to get to Rioja's side; had she still not given up?

Madeline linked arms with her. "Where's Carola?"

"She won't get lost." Tanja was clearly in a bad mood.

"She went back to the dressing room," said Rioja. "She must find film-making as boring as you do, Madeline."

"I think it's absolutely fascinating." Tanja gave Rioja a downright lascivious glance.

But Rioja didn't seem impressed. "Then you should do like your friend Carola."

"Why? What is she doing?"

"She did Consuela's hair this morning."

Tanja opened her mouth; Madeline also seemed to be surprised. "And?

"Consuela's hairdresser is taking her under her wing: Pilar has made friends with some people here and maybe she can do something to get her out of her salon."

"Hardly!" Madeline shook her head regretfully. "Carola hasn't finished her apprenticeship yet."

Tanja laughed. "They won't have a job for her immediately either. But that might be a start on getting a foot in the door in the long run."

"You see!" Rioja patted her back and Tanja blushed.

"What do I see? There is no job for me here."

"And what are you doing right now?" He pulled her leg; that was crystal clear. But she didn't seem to notice.

Micky smirked. "Are you planning your star careers now?" If he returned to the tone that usually prevailed between him and Tanja, maybe they would find their way back to normal without having to talk about their childish behaviors.

"As what?" asked Lydia.

"As what, Tanja?" Madeline grinned at her. "Another Western?"

"I doubt that enough Westerns are being shot here."

"Dance films are no longer fashionable either," said Lydia.

"Musicals." Rioja looked like he was serious about it. "Consuela has an offer for next year."

"Here in Babelsberg?" Tanja stopped. "That would be cool."

"Why?" Madeline's gaze expressed the same mistrust that awakened in Micky. "Because of Carola?

"Of course because of Carola. If she has completed her apprenticeship by then..." Only Carola had just failed again in theory; but this Pilar didn't need to know that.

However, Tanja got a highly suspicious glitter in her eyes. Was there any guarantee that Rioja would still be the faithful husband next year?

"Then you will surely be here again, too," Micky said to him. He just wanted to know what he had to expect.

Rioja shook his head. "We rarely have work together." He burst out laughing. "I can neither sing nor dance.

"And what are you doing with us right now?" Madeline smirked.

Tanja pulled at Rioja's arm to get his attention. "Wouldn't you have to come because you'd have to take care of your child?"

"That's why I didn't take any engagement for the same time." He grinned. "I can afford to set the shooting dates."

Behind them a bicycle suddenly rang, continuously and piercingly. One of the script supervisors cycled towards them with a deep red head, pedaling vigorously. "Manolo!" She gasped.

He stepped up to her and caught her as she abruptly braked in front of him. She got off, he grabbed the bike and chased back the way the script supervisor had just come.

"What's the matter?" Tanja looked around bewildered.

"What do you think! It's a good thing Chris is still in the studio." Madeline grabbed the script supervisor's arm. "Will you show me the way?" She urged the woman to hurry.

"So what's going on? Madeline behaves as if it's already burning. That's only planned for the afternoon."

"But Tanja!" Micky reached out to her. "Let's have a bite to eat. We certainly don't need to wait for them anymore." He frowned. "Hopefully that doesn't mean the afternoon shooting's off."

Ana looked puzzled from one to the other.

"Consuela," Micky said.

"*¡Dios!*" Ana broke away from him and ran after Madeline.

"You mean she's having her baby? Now?" Well, finally Tanja understood too. "Then surely they'll send us straight home." Strangely enough, it didn't sound as if she was sorry about it.

"Hardly. Manolo is a professional, isn't he?" Lydia put a hand on her belly. "I wouldn't expect Sakir to do that either."

Tanja's eyes became huge; then she began to giggle. "That's why you got sick this morning," she pushed out snorting.

Micky stared for a moment at Lydia's hand: Lydia was pregnant. But what was so funny about it? Women – who would understand their train of thoughts. "Are we going to the canteen now?" Again he stuck out his arm.

Lydia linked arms with him and then reached for Tanja's hand. Of course, we're going to eat now."

"And we'll make sure you eat for two." In high spirits Tanja swung Lydia's hand. Finally her good mood seemed to be back. She went half a step ahead so that she could look at him. "How about you, actually? Do you like children?"

"That depends."

"On what?"

"On whose children they are." He was overcome by an impulse of boldness. "If they were yours, I would love them."

Lydia let them both go and pushed them towards each other laughing. "Well, it's time you settle it for good."

Tanja's eyes glittered. Those weren't tears, were they?

"Oh Micky!" She put her arms around his neck and her face on his cheek. "You idiot!"

That she always had to have the last word.

THE END

***

If you liked this novel, please recommend it to others. Recommendations and reviews help others to find books worth reading.

If you want to know, when more of my books are available in English, sign up to my newsletter.

***

Quick, quick, slow – Lietzensee Dance Club
– Dance Novels –

The idea for these "Dance Novels" was developed by the author group "Schreibwerk". The stories are set in Germany in a fictitious Berlin dance club during the first decade of this century.

Each book in the series can be read as a stand-alone.

At present, only Annemarie Nikolaus is getting her novels translated. In addition to English, currently available are translations into Italian, Spanish and Greek.

The Granddaughter.

Madeline Lagrange loses her heart to square dancing – and to the group's caller. Chris Rinehart, the caller of the "Lietzensee Dance Club", falls for Madeline. Yet out of a sense of responsibility he denies her his feelings. While Madeline tries to seduce Chris with all the intransigence of her seventeen years, her grandfather wants to expel him from the club.

Paperback edition ISBN 9781795425490

Back onto the Dance Floor.

After sixteen years, Friederike Lagrange dares to return to the dance floor for the first time: A serious car accident had forced her to give up competition dancing. Instead, dance became her research topic and she made a career as a professor in history.

A colleague becomes her new partner because her husband George doesn't want to take part in a simple dance circle like a beginner: It would be beneath his dignity as chairman of the Lietzensee Dance Club. But he supports her when she wants to shoot a film about the dances of the Baroque with the square dancers and the Latin formation of the club. Then suddenly he wants to dance the Baroque dances with her himself.

Friederike is faced with a dilemma: Since the accident she has longed to be able to dance with her husband again one day. But she also doesn't want to disappoint her colleague. Can she find a way out that doesn't offend either of them?

Furthermore:

Die Enkelin. Also in English, Italian, Spanish and Greek.
Zurück aufs Parkett. Also in English and Italian.
Flirt mit einem Star. Also in Italian and Spanish.

From other authors

Tine Sprandel: **Der Treppensturz** and **Nele**.
Marion Pletzer: **Tanz bei offenen Türen**
Evelyn Sperber-Hummel: **Liebe tanzt Rumba**

About the author

Annemarie Nikolaus began writing literary fiction in 2001. Her first novel was published in 2005. She's now an independent author.

She was born in Hessia/Germany and lived in Northern Italy for 20 years. In 2010, she moved to the Auvergne region in France with her daughter.

After studying psychology, journalism, politics and history, she worked as a psychotherapist, political advisor, journalist, editor and translator.

You can find Annemarie on Facebook
www.facebook.com/AnnemarieNikolaus.Autorin
and Twitter: http://twitter.com/AnneNikolaus

Publications:

In English:

Magical Stories. Short stories for children. Paperback edition ISBN 9781479157037.

Radiant Hope. Illustrated science-fiction story. Paperback edition ISBN 9781484977163.

Past Crimes. Historical crime short stories. Paperback edition ISBN 9781507136744

Silenced. Short thriller. Paperback edition ISBN 9781507176238

Deceased. Short Stories. Paperback edition ISBN 9781507190371.

Aquitaine: The End of a War. *"By The Wayside..."* series. Paperback edition ISBN 9781507141861

The Granddaughter. *"Quick, quick, slow – Lietzensee Dance Club"* series. Paperback edition ISBN 9781795425490

Back onto the Dance Floor. *"Quick, quick, slow – Lietzensee Dance Club"* series. Paperback edition ISBN 9781796510287

In German:

Novels and short stories

Historical

Königliche Republik. *"Welt in Flammen"* series. Historical novel. Paperback edition ISBN 9781477531143

Verjährt. Historical crime short stories. Paperback edition ISBN 9781484020838.

Fantasy

Die Piratin. *"Drachenwelt"* series. Fantasy novel. Paperback edition ISBN 9781533620705

Das Feuerpferd. Fantasy novel, together with Monique Lhoir und Sabine Abel. Paperback edition ISBN 9781461134909

Magische Geschichten. Short stories for children and adults. Paperback edition ISBN 9781478172987

Renntag in Kruschar. *"Drachenwelt"* series. Fantasy anthology. E-Book only

Leuchtende Hoffnung. A Science Fiction novel in Advent calendar form. Paperback edition ISBN 9781478319580

Crime

Ustica. Short story thriller. Paperback edition ISBN 9781484963197 Paperback with voucher for the e-Book.

Tot. Short stories. Paperback edition ISBN 9781548392932

Verjährt. (see above)

Romance

Die Enkelin. *"Quick, quick, slow - Tanzclub Lietzensee"* series. Love story. Paperback edition ISBN 9781484967744.

Flirt mit einem Star. *"Quick, quick, slow - Tanzclub Liet-zensee"* series. Love story. Paperback edition ISBN 9781512049220

Zurück aufs Parkett. *"Quick, quick, slow - Tanzclub Liet-zensee"* series. Story of love and marriage. Paperback edition ISBN 9781490904832

Non-fiction

Tourist attractions

Aquitanien: Das Ende eines Krieges. *"Am Rande des Weges ..."* series. Paperback edition ISBN 9781533161758

Background series on literature and books

Suche Reisebegleitung. *Fliegende Blätter.* Paperback edition ISBN 9781499608427

Junge Welten. *Fliegende Blätter.* Paperback edition ISBN 9781500971991